MILLY-
MOLLY-
MANDY'S
FAMILY

Publisher's Note

*The stories in this collection are reproduced in the form in which they appeared
upon first publication in the UK by George G. Harrap & Co. Ltd.
All spellings remain consistent with these original editions*

KINGFISHER
An imprint of Kingfisher Publications Plc
New Penderel House, 283–288 High Holborn
London WC1V 7HZ
www.kingfisherpub.com

First published by Kingfisher 2005
2 4 6 8 10 9 7 5 3

The stories in this collection first appeared in
Milly-Molly-Mandy Stories (1928)
More of Milly-Molly-Mandy (1929)
Milly-Molly-Mandy & Co (1955)
published by George G. Harrap & Co. Ltd.

Text and illustrations copyright © Joyce Lankester Brisley,
1928, 1929, 1955
Cover illustrations copyright © Clara Vulliamy 2000

A CIP catalogue record for this book is available from the British Library.

ISBN 0 7534 1124 5
Printed in India
2TS/0705/THOM/HBM(PICA)/115GSM/F

MILLY-MOLLY-MANDY'S

FAMILY

JOYCE LANKESTER BRISLEY

KINGFISHER

CONTENTS

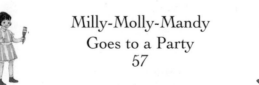

MILLY-MOLLY-MANDY
GOES ERRANDS

ONCE UPON A TIME there was a little girl.

She had a Father, and a Mother, and a Grandpa, and a Grandma, and an Uncle, and an Aunty; and they all lived together in a nice white cottage with a thatched roof.

This little girl had short hair, and short legs, and short frocks (pink-and-white-striped cotton in summer, and red serge in winter). But her name wasn't short at all. It was Millicent Margaret Amanda. But Father and Mother and Grandpa and Grandma and Uncle and Aunty couldn't very well call out "Millicent Margaret Amanda!" every time they wanted her, so they shortened it to 'Milly-Molly-Mandy,' which is quite easy to say.

Now everybody in the nice white cottage

5

with the thatched roof had some particular job to do – even Milly-Molly-Mandy.

Father grew vegetables in the big garden by the cottage. Mother cooked the dinners and did the washing. Grandpa took the vegetables to market in his little pony-cart. Grandma knitted socks and mittens and nice warm woollies for them all. Uncle kept cows (to give them milk) and chickens (to give them eggs). Aunty sewed frocks and shirts for them, and did the sweeping and dusting.

And Milly-Molly-Mandy, what did she do?

Well, Milly-Molly-Mandy's legs were short, as I've told you, but they were very lively, just right for running errands. So Milly-Molly-Mandy was quite busy, fetching and carrying things, and taking messages.

One fine day Milly-Molly-Mandy was in the garden playing with Toby the dog, when Father poked his head out from the other side of a big row of beans, and said:

"Milly-Molly-Mandy, run down to Mr

Moggs' cottage and ask for the trowel he borrowed from me!"

So Milly-Molly-Mandy said, "Yes, Farver!" and ran in to get her hat.

At the kitchen door was Mother, with a basket of eggs in her hand. And when she saw Milly-Molly-Mandy she said:

"Milly-Molly-Mandy, run down to Mrs Moggs and give her these eggs. She's got visitors."

So Milly-Molly-Mandy said, "Yes, Muvver!" and took the basket. "Trowel for Farver, eggs for Muvver," she thought to herself.

Then Grandpa came up and said:

"Milly-Molly-Mandy, please get me a ball of string from Miss Muggins' shop – here's a penny."

So Milly-Molly-Mandy said, "Yes, Grandpa!" and took the penny, thinking to herself, "Trowel for Farver, eggs for Muvver, string for Grandpa."

As she passed through the kitchen Grandma, who was sitting in her armchair knitting said:

"Milly-Molly-Mandy, will you get me a skein of red wool? Here's a sixpence."

So Milly-Molly-Mandy said, "Yes, Grandma!" and took the sixpence. "Trowel for Farver, eggs for Muvver, string for Grandpa, red wool for Grandma," she whispered over to herself.

As she went into the passage Uncle came striding up in a hurry.

"Oh, Milly-Molly-Mandy," said Uncle, "run like a good girl to Mr Blunt's shop, and tell him I'm waiting for the chicken-feed he promised to send!"

So Milly-Molly-Mandy said, "Yes, Uncle!" and thought to herself, "Trowel for Farver, eggs for Muvver, string for Grandpa, red wool for Grandma, chicken-feed for Uncle."

As she got her hat off the peg Aunty called from the parlour where she was dusting:

"Is that Milly-Molly-Mandy? Will you get me a packet of needles, dear? Here's a penny!"

So Milly-Molly-Mandy said, "Yes, Aunty!" and took the penny, thinking to herself, "Trowel for Farver, eggs for Muvver, string for Grandpa, red wool for Grandma, chicken-feed for Uncle, needles for Aunty, and I do hope there won't be anything more!"

GRANDPA · GRANDMA · FATHER · MOTHER · UNCLE · AUNTY · MILLY-MOLLY-MANDY.

But there was nothing else, so Milly-Molly-Mandy started out down the path. When she came to the gate Toby the dog capered up, looking very excited at the thought of a walk. But Milly-Molly-Mandy eyed him solemnly, and said:

"Trowel for Farver, eggs for Muvver, string for Grandpa, red wool for Grandma, chicken-feed for Uncle, needles for Aunty. No, Toby, you mustn't come now, I've too much to think about. But I promise to take you for a walk when I come back!"

So she left Toby on the other side of the gate, and set off down the road, with the basket and the pennies and the sixpence.

Presently she met a little friend, and the little friend said:

"Hello, Milly-Molly-Mandy! I've got a new see-saw! Do come on it with me!"

But Milly-Molly-Mandy looked at her solemnly and said:

"Trowel for Farver, eggs for Muvver, string for Grandpa, red wool for Grandma, chicken-feed for Uncle, needles for Aunty. No, Susan, I can't come now, I'm busy. But I'd like to come when I get back – after I've taken Toby for a walk."

So Milly-Molly-Mandy went on her way with the basket and the pennies and the six-pence.

Soon she came to the Moggs' cottage.

"Please, Mrs Moggs, can I have the trowel for Farver? And here are some eggs from Muvver!" she said.

Mrs Moggs was very much obliged indeed for the eggs, and fetched the trowel and a piece of seed-cake for Milly-Molly-Mandy's own self. And Milly-Molly-Mandy went on her way with the empty basket.

Next she came to Miss Muggins' little shop.

"Please, Miss Muggins, can I have a ball of string for Grandpa and a skein of red wool for Grandma?"

So Miss Muggins put the string and the wool into Milly-Molly-Mandy's basket, and took a penny and a sixpence in exchange. So that left Milly-Molly-Mandy with one penny. And Milly-Molly-Mandy couldn't remember what that penny was for.

"Sweeties, perhaps?" said Miss Muggins,

glancing at the row of glass bottles on the shelf.

But Milly-Molly-Mandy shook her head.

"No," she said, "and it can't be chicken-feed for Uncle, because that would be more than a penny, only I haven't got to pay for it."

"It must be sweeties!" said Miss Muggins.

"No," said Milly-Molly-Mandy, "but I'll remember soon. Good morning, Miss Muggins!"

So Milly-Molly-Mandy went on to Mr Blunt's and gave him Uncle's message, and then she sat down on the doorstep and thought what that penny could be for.

And she couldn't remember.

But she remembered one thing: "It's for Aunty," she thought, "and I love Aunty." And she thought for just a little while longer. Then suddenly she sprang up and went back to Miss Muggins' shop.

"I've remembered!" she said. "It's needles for Aunty!"

So Miss Muggins put the packet of needles into the basket, and took the penny, and Milly-Molly-Mandy set off for home.

"That's a good little messenger to remember all those things!" said Mother, when she got there. They were just going to begin dinner. "I thought you were only going with my eggs!"

"She went for my trowel!" said Father.

"And my string!" said Grandpa.

"And my wool!" said Grandma.

"And my chicken-feed!" said Uncle.

"And my needles!" said Aunty.

Then they all laughed; and Grandpa, feeling in his pocket, said:

"Well, here's another errand for you – go and get yourself some sweeties!"

So after dinner Toby had a nice walk and his mistress got her sweets. And then Milly-Molly-Mandy and little-friend-Susan had a lovely time on the see-saw, chatting and eating raspberry-drops, and feeling very happy and contented indeed.

MILLY-MOLLY-MANDY'S
MOTHER GOES AWAY

ONCE UPON A TIME Milly-Molly-Mandy's
Mother went away from the nice white cottage
with the thatched roof for a whole fortnight's
holiday.

Milly-Molly-Mandy's Mother hardly ever
went away for holidays – in fact, Milly-Molly-
Mandy could only remember her going away
once before, a long time ago (and that was
only for two days).

Mrs Hooker, Mother's friend in the next
town, invited her. Mrs Hooker wanted to have
a holiday by the sea, and she didn't want to go
alone, as it isn't so much fun, so she wrote and
asked Mother to come with her.

When Mother read the letter first, she said it
was very kind of Mrs Hooker, but she couldn't

possibly go, as she didn't see how ever Father
and Grandpa and Grandma and Uncle and
Aunty and Milly-Molly-Mandy would get on
without her to cook dinners for them, and
wash clothes for them, and see after things.

But Aunty said she could manage to do the
cooking and the washing, somehow; and
Grandma said she could do Aunty's sweeping
and dusting; and Milly-Molly-Mandy said she
would help all she knew how; and Father and
Grandpa and Uncle said they wouldn't be
fussy, or make any more work than they could
help.

And then they all begged Mother to write to
Mrs Hooker and accept. So Mother did, and
she was quite excited (and so
was Milly-Molly-Mandy for
her!).

Then Mother bought a
new hat and a blouse
and a sunshade, and
she packed them in her
trunk with all her best
things (Milly-Molly-Mandy helping).

And then she kissed Grandpa and Grandma

15

and Uncle and Aunty goodbye, and hugged Milly-Molly-Mandy. And then Father drove her in the pony-trap to the next town to the station to meet Mrs Hooker and go with her by train to the sea. (She kissed Father goodbye at the station.)

And so Father and Grandpa and Grandma and Uncle and Aunty and Milly-Molly-Mandy had to manage as best they could in the nice white cottage with the thatched roof for a whole fortnight without Mother. It did feel queer.

Milly-Molly-Mandy kept forgetting, and she would run in from school to tell Mother all about something, and find it was Aunty in Mother's apron bending over the kitchen stove instead of Mother herself. And Father would put his head in at the kitchen door and say, "Polly, will you –" and then suddenly remember that "Polly" was having a lovely holiday by the sea (Polly was Mother's other name, of course). And they felt so pleased when they remembered, but it did seem a long time to wait till she came back.

Then one day Father said, "I've got a plan!

Don't you think it would be a good idea, while Polly's away, if we were to . . . "

And then Father told them all his plan; and Grandpa and Grandma and Uncle and Aunty thought it was a very fine plan, and so did Milly-Molly-Mandy. (But I mustn't tell you what it was, because it was to be a surprise, and you know how secrets do get about once you start telling them! But I'll just tell you this, that they made the kitchen and the scullery and the passage outside the kitchen most dreadfully untidy, so that nothing was in its proper place, and they had to have meals like picnics, only not so nice – though Milly-Molly-Mandy thought it quite fun.)

Well, they all worked awfully hard at the plan in all their spare time, and nobody really minded having things all upset, because it was such fun to think how surprised Mother would be when she came back!

Then another day Grandpa said: "There's something I've been meaning to do for some time, to please Polly; I guess it would be a good plan to set about it now. It is . . . "

And then Grandpa told them all his plan;

and Father and Grandma and Uncle and Aunty thought it was a very fine plan, and so did Milly-Molly-Mandy. (But I mustn't tell you what it was! – though I will just tell you this, that Grandpa was very busy digging up things in the garden and planting them again, and bringing things home in a box at the back of the pony-trap on market day. And Milly-Molly-Mandy helped him all she could.)

Then Uncle had a plan, and Father and Grandpa and Grandma and Aunty thought it was a very fine plan, and so did Milly-Molly-Mandy. (It's a secret, remember! – but I will just tell you this, that Uncle got a lot of bits of wood and nails and a hammer, and he was very busy in the evening after he had shut up his chickens for the night – which he called "putting them to bed.")

Then Grandma and Aunty had a plan, and Father and Grandpa and Uncle thought it was a very fine plan, and so did Milly-Molly-Mandy. (But I can only just tell you this, that Grandma and Aunty and Milly-Molly-Mandy, who helped too, made themselves very untidy and dusty indeed, and nobody had any cakes for tea at all that week, what with Aunty being so busy and the kitchen so upset. But nobody really minded, because it was such fun to think how pleased Mother would be when she came back!)

And then the day arrived when Mother was to return home!

They had all been working so hard in the nice white cottage with the thatched roof that the two weeks had simply flown. But they had just managed to get things straight again, and Aunty had baked a cake for tea, and Milly-Molly-Mandy had put flowers in all the vases.

When Father helped Mother down from the pony-trap it almost didn't seem as if it could be Mother at first; but of course it was! – only she had on her new hat, and she was so brown with sitting on the beach, and so very pleased to be home again!

She kissed them all round and just hugged Milly-Molly-Mandy!

And then they led her indoors.

And directly Mother got inside the doorway – she saw a beautiful new passage, all clean and painted! And she was surprised!

Then she went upstairs and took off her things, and came back down into the kitchen. And directly Mother got inside the door – she saw a beautiful new kitchen, all clean and sunny, with the ceiling whitewashed and the walls freshly painted! And she was surprised!

When they had had tea (Aunty's cake was very good, though not quite like Mother's) she helped to carry the cups and plates out into the scullery. And directly Mother got through the doorway – she saw a beautiful new scullery, all clean and white-washed! And she was surprised!

She put the cups down on the draining board, and directly she looked out of the window – she saw a beautiful new flower garden

And she was surprised!

just outside, and a rustic trellis-work hiding the dustbin. And she was surprised!

Then Mother went upstairs to unpack. And when her trunk was cleared, Grandpa carried it up to the attic and Mother went first to open the door. And directly she opened it – Mother saw a beautifully tidy, spring-cleaned attic!

And then Mother couldn't say anything, but that they were all very dear, naughty people to have worked so hard while she was being lazy! And Father and Grandpa and Grandma and Uncle and Aunty and Milly-Molly-Mandy were all very pleased, and said they liked being naughty!

Then Mother brought out the presents she had got for them. And what do you think Milly-Molly-Mandy's present was (besides some shells which Mother had picked up on the sand)?

It was a beautiful little blue dressing-gown, which Mother had sewed and sewed for her while she sat on the beach and under her new sunshade with Mrs Hooker listening to the waves splashing!

Then Father and Grandpa and Grandma

and Uncle and Aunty and Milly-Molly-Mandy all said Mother was very naughty to have worked when she might have been having a nice lazy time!

But Mother said she liked being naughty too! – and Milly-Molly-Mandy was so pleased with her new little blue dressing-gown that she couldn't help wearing it straight away!

And then Mother put on her apron and insisted on setting to work to make them something nice for supper, so that she should feel she was really at home.

For it had been a perfect holiday, said Mother, but it was really like having another one to come home again to them all at the nice white cottage with the thatched roof.

MILLY-MOLLY-MANDY
GOES TO A CONCERT

ONCE UPON A TIME Milly-Molly-Mandy was going to a grown-up concert with Father and Mother and Grandpa and Grandma and Uncle and Aunty. (They had all got their tickets.)

It was to be held in the Village Institute at seven o'clock, and it wouldn't be over until quite nine o'clock, which was lovely and late for Milly-Molly-Mandy. But you see this wasn't like an ordinary concert, where people you didn't know sang and did things.

It was a quite extra specially important concert, for Aunty was going to play on the piano on the platform, and the young lady who helped Mrs Hubble in her baker's shop was going to sing, and some other people whom

Milly-Molly-Mandy had heard spoken of were going to do things too. So it was very exciting indeed.

Aunty had a new mauve silk scarf for her neck, and a newly trimmed hat, and her handkerchief was sprinkled with the lavender water that Milly-Molly-Mandy had given her last Christmas.

Milly-Molly-Mandy felt so proud that it was being used for such a special occasion. (Aunty put a drop on Milly-Molly-Mandy's own handkerchief too.)

When they had all got into their best clothes and shoes, they said goodbye to Toby the dog and Topsy the cat, and started off for the village – Father and Mother and Grandpa and Grandma and Uncle and Aunty and Milly-Molly-Mandy. And they as nearly as possible forgot to take the tickets with them off the mantelpiece! But Mother remembered just in time.

There were several people already in their seats when Father and Mother and Grandpa and Grandma and Uncle and Aunty and Milly-Molly-Mandy got to the Institute. Mr and Mrs Hubble and the young lady who helped them were just in front, and Mr and Mrs Blunt and Mr and Mrs Moggs (little-friend-Susan's father and mother) were just behind (Billy Blunt and little-friend-Susan weren't there, but then they hadn't got an aunty who was going to play on the platform, so it wasn't so important for them to be up late).

The platform looked very nice, with plants in crinkly green paper. And the piano was standing there, all ready for Aunty. People were coming in very fast, and it wasn't long before the hall was full, everybody was talking and rustling programmes. Then people started clapping, and Milly-Molly-Mandy saw that some ladies and gentlemen with violins and things were going up steps on to the platform, with very solemn faces. A lady hit one or two notes on the piano, and the people with violins played a lot of funny noises without taking any notice of each other (Mother said they were "tuning up"). And then they all started off playing properly, and the concert had begun.

Milly-Molly-Mandy did enjoy it. She clapped as hard as ever she could, and so did everybody else, when the music stopped. After that people sang one at a time, or a lot at a time, or played the piano, and one man sang a funny song (which made Milly-Molly-Mandy laugh and everybody else too).

But Milly-Molly-Mandy was longing for the time to come for Aunty to play.

She was just asking Mother in a whisper when Aunty was going to play, when she heard a queer little sound, just like a dog walking on the wooden floor. And she looked round and saw people at the back of the hall glancing down here and there, smiling and pointing.

And presently what should she feel but a

cold, wet nose on her leg, and what should she see but a white, furry object coming out from under her chair.

And there was Toby the dog (without a ticket), looking just as pleased with himself as he could be for having found them!

Milly-Molly-Mandy was very shocked at him and so was Mother. She said "Naughty Toby!" in a whisper, and Father pushed him under the seat and made him lie down. They couldn't disturb the concert by taking him out just then.

So there Toby the dog stayed and heard the concert without a ticket; and now and then Milly-Molly-Mandy put down her hand and Toby the dog licked it and half got up to wag his tail. But Father said, "Ssh!" so Milly-

Molly-Mandy put her hand back in her lap, and Toby the dog settled down again. But they liked being near each other.

Then the time came for the young lady who helped Mrs Hubble to sing, and Aunty to play for her. So the young lady got up and dropped her handbag, and Aunty got up and dropped her music (it made Toby the dog jump!). But they were picked up again, and then Aunty and the young lady went up on to the platform.

And who do you think went up with them?

Why, Toby the dog! Looking just as if he thought Aunty had meant him to follow!

Everybody laughed, and Aunty pointed to Toby the dog to go down again. But Toby the dog didn't seem to understand, and he got behind the piano and wouldn't come out.

So Aunty had to play and the young lady to sing with Toby the dog peeping out now and then from behind the piano, and everybody tried not to notice him, lest it should make them laugh.

But still Aunty played beautifully and the young lady sang, and Milly-Molly-Mandy clapped as hard as she could, and so did everybody else when the song was finished. In fact, they all clapped so loud that Toby the dog gave a surprised bark, and everybody laughed again.

They had another try then to get Toby the dog off the platform, but Toby the dog wouldn't come.

Then Father said, "Milly-Molly-Mandy, you go and see if you can get him."

So Milly-Molly-Mandy slipped off her seat, past the people's knees, and climbed up the steps on to the platform (in front of all the audience).

And she said, "Toby, come here!" round the corner of the piano, and Toby the dog put out his nose and sniffed her hand, and Milly-Molly-Mandy was able to catch hold of his collar and pull him out.

She walked right across the platform with Toby the dog in her arms, and everybody laughed, and somebody (I think it was the Blacksmith) called out, "Bravo! Encore!" and clapped.

And Milly-Molly-Mandy (feeling very hot) hurried down the steps, with Toby the dog

She walked right across the platform

licking all over one side of her cheek and hair.

There was only a little bit of the concert to come after that, so Milly-Molly-Mandy stood at the back of the hall with Toby the dog till it was finished. Then everybody started crowding to the door. Most of them smiled at Milly-Molly-Mandy and Toby the dog as they stood waiting for Father and Mother and Grandpa and Grandma and Uncle and Aunty to come.

Mr Jakes the Postman, passing with Mrs Jakes, said, "Well, well! I didn't expect to see you turning out a public character just yet awhile, young lady." And Milly-Molly-Mandy laughed with Mr Jakes.

Then Mr Rudge, the Blacksmith, passed, and he said solemnly, "You and Toby gave us a very fine performance indeed. If I'd known beforehand I'd have sent you up a bouquet each." Milly-Molly-Mandy liked the Blacksmith – he was a nice man.

"Well," said Aunty, as they all walked home together in the dark, "I think if we'd known Toby was going to perform up on the platform tonight, we'd have given him a bath and a new collar first!"

MILLY-MOLLY-MANDY
AND THE GOLDEN WEDDING

ONCE UPON A TIME Milly-Molly-Mandy
was busy dipping fingers of bread-and-butter
into her boiled egg at supper-time, and listening while Father and Mother and Grandpa
and Grandma and Uncle and Aunty talked.

They were counting how long it was that
Grandpa and Grandma had been married.
And it was a very long time indeed – nearly
fifty years!

Grandma said: "Our Golden Wedding –
next month!"

Milly-Molly-Mandy was
very interested, though she
did not know what a Golden
Wedding was. But it
sounded rather grand.

"Do you have to be

married all over again when you've been married fifty years?" she asked.

"No," said Mother; "its more like having a very special sort of birthday. When you've been married twenty-five years you have a Silver Wedding Day, and people give you silver presents. But when you've been married fifty years it's a Golden one. We shall have to think what we can do to celebrate Grandpa's and Grandma's Golden Wedding Day. Dear me!"

Milly-Molly-Mandy whispered: "Do we have to give golden presents to Grandpa and Grandma?"

Mother whispered back: "We shall have to think what we can do about it, Milly-Molly-Mandy. But there are different sorts of gold, you know – sunshine and buttercups and, well, little girls, even, can be good as gold sometimes! We shall have to think."

Grandpa (eating his kipper) heard their whisperings, and said: "If Milly-Molly-Mandy promises to be as good as gold that day you can just wrap her up in tissue-paper and hand her over. She'll do for a Golden Wedding present!"

34

But Milly-Molly-Mandy wouldn't promise to be as good as all that!

She did wonder, though, what sort of gold presents Father and Mother and Uncle and Aunty would be giving to Grandpa and Grandma. And she wondered too, very much, what sort of a gold present she herself could give. It was important to think of something very special for such a special occasion.

She talked with little-friend-Susan and Billy Blunt about it before school next morning.

Little-friend-Susan said: "I'd like to give a present too. But I haven't enough money."

Billy Blunt said: "I'd be rich if I could give anybody a gold present!"

"But it doesn't always have to be that sort of present," Milly-Molly-Mandy told them. "There's good-as-gold, if we could think of something like that. Only I can't think what."

And then they met others on their way in to school, and had other things to think about.

A few days later Billy Blunt showed Milly-Molly-Mandy a crumpled bit of newspaper he had in his pocket, and made her read it. It was something about a golden-jubilee concert somewhere. Milly-Molly-Mandy couldn't think why Billy Blunt bothered to keep it.

"Plain as your nose," said Billy Blunt. "Golden jubilee means fifty years, like your Golden Wedding business. They're having a concert to celebrate. Thought you might be interested."

And then, suddenly, Milly-Molly-Mandy was very interested.

"You mean *we* might do something like that for Grandpa and Grandma? Oh, Billy! what a good idea. What can we do?"

But Billy Blunt only said: "Oh, it was just an idea."

And he went off to exchange foreign stamps

with a friend of his, Timmy Biggs. So Milly-Molly-Mandy looked for little-friend-Susan to tell her.

"But what could we do for a concert?" asked little-friend-Susan. "We can't play or anything."

But Milly-Molly-Mandy said (like Mother): "We shall have to think, Susan!"

The Golden Wedding meant a lot of thinking for everybody – Father and Mother and Uncle and Aunty as well.

Mother had the first idea. She said (while Grandpa and Grandma were out of the way): "I shall make a big golden wedding-cake, iced with yellow icing, and trimmed with gold hearts and a gold paper frill. We'll have a Golden Wedding tea-party!"

Father and Uncle and Aunty and Milly-Molly-Mandy thought that was a grand idea!

After school next morning Milly-Molly-Mandy and little-friend-Susan and Billy Blunt looked in Miss Muggins's shop window to see if there was anything interesting there besides socks and dusters and underclothes.

"There's a little gold bell with a handle on that shelf – see," said Milly-Molly-Mandy, "and pins with gold heads."

"Those yellow pencils with gold tops look quite cheap," said little-friend-Susan, "and that Happy Returns card with gold print!"

(Really, there seemed quite a number of gold things if you kept your eyes open!)

Billy Blunt looked carefully, but said nothing.

"Have you thought what you can do at the concert?" Milly-Molly-Mandy asked him.

"What concert?" said Billy Blunt.

"Our Golden Wedding concert, of course!" said Milly-Molly-Mandy.

"Huh!" said Billy Blunt. And then he said: "Better call a meeting and make plans."

"Ooh, yes let's!" said Milly-Molly-Mandy and little-friend-Susan together. And Milly-Molly-Mandy added, "Somewhere secret, where Grandpa and Grandma won't know!"

Billy Blunt said they might come to his place after tea on Saturday; his folk would be in the corn-shop, and they could plan in private there.

So directly after tea on Saturday Milly-Molly-Mandy met little-friend-Susan at the Moggs's gate, and they ran together down to the village, and through the gate at the side of the corn-shop, and up the garden path into the Blunts's house.

"Oh, it's you," said Billy Blunt (as if he wasn't expecting them).

Milly-Molly-Mandy hadn't seen inside the Blunts's sitting-room before, only in the corn-shop. It was small and rather dark, but very cosy, with a thick red cloth on the table.

"Sit down," said Billy Blunt. "The meeting's begun. I'm President, as it's my house."

"But it's *my* Golden Wedding," Milly-Molly-Mandy told him.

They laughed at that (because Milly-Molly-Mandy didn't look over fifty), and then they felt more at home.

Billy Blunt thumped on the table, and said, "Order, now!"

And they settled down to thinking what they could do about a concert.

They couldn't play the piano, though there was one which Aunty played on at the nice white cottage with the thatched roof (where, of course, Milly-Molly-Mandy lived). Billy Blunt had an old mouth-organ, but it was broken. And little-friend-Susan had a dulcimer, but her baby sister played with it and half the notes were gone.

"Then we'll have to make up things," said Milly-Molly-Mandy. "I can play a comb and tissue-paper!"

"Saucepan lids make awfully nice clappers," said little-friend-Susan.

Billy Blunt reached down and picked up the shovel and poker from the fireplace and started hitting them together, till Milly-Molly-Mandy and little-friend-Susan shouted at him that Grandpa and Grandma wouldn't like that one bit! So then he put the shovel to his shoulder and sawed up and down it with the poker, singing, "Tweedle-tweedle-tweedle," exactly as if he were playing the violin!

Milly-Molly-Mandy and little-friend-Susan
did wish they had thought of that first!

"Well!" said Milly-Molly-Mandy. "We can
have a band, and then we'll recite something.
What can we say?"

"Let's write a poem," said little-friend-Susan.

So they thought awhile. And then Milly-
Molly-Mandy said:

"Dear Grandpa and Grandma, we want to say
We wish you a happy Golden Wedding Day!"

"Bit long," said Billy Blunt.

"But it rhymes," said Milly-Molly-Mandy.

"Yes, it does," said little-friend-Susan.
"Can't we get in something about Many
Happy Returns?"

"Can you have returns of Golden Weddings?" asked Milly-Molly-Mandy. "I thought
you only had one."

"You could have one every fifty years, I
expect," said Billy Blunt. "You'd be a bit old
by next time, though!"

"Well, we'd like Grandpa and Grandma to
have heaps of Golden Weddings, till they were
millions of years old!" said Milly-Molly-Mandy.

So they thought again, and added:

"We want you to know our heart all burns
To wish you Many Happy Returns."

Billy Blunt wrote it down on a piece of paper, and while the others tried to think up some more he went on scribbling for a bit. Then he read out loudly:

"We hope you like this little stunt,
Done by Mister William Blunt!"

There was a lot of shouting at that, as the others of course, wanted to have their names in too! They made so much noise that Mrs Blunt looked in from the corn-shop to see what was up.

Billy Blunt said: "Sorry, Mum!" And they went on with the meeting in whispers.

Well, the great day arrived.

Only a few special people were invited to the party, but there seemed quite a crowd – Grandpa and Grandma, Father and Mother, Uncle and Aunty, Mr Moggs and Mrs Moggs (their nearest neighbours), little-friend-Susan and Baby Moggs (who couldn't be left

Mother and Aunty between them had prepared a splendid tea

behind), Billy Blunt (by special request), and, of course, Milly-Molly-Mandy.

Mother and Aunty between them had prepared a splendid tea, with the big decorated Golden Wedding cake in the centre, and buttered scones, and brown and white bread-and-butter and honey, and apricot jam, and lemon-curd tarts, and orange buns (everything as nearly golden-coloured as possible, of course) arranged round it.

But before Mother filled the teapot everybody had to give Grandpa and Grandma their golden presents. (Milly-Molly-Mandy and little-friend-Susan and Billy Blunt were all very interested to see what everyone was giving!)

Well, Mr and Mrs Moggs gave a beautiful gilt basket tied with gold ribbons, full of lovely yellow chrysanthemums.

Father and Mother gave a pair of real gold cuff-links to Grandpa, and a little gold locket (with a photo of Milly-Molly-Mandy inside) to Grandma.

Uncle and Aunty gave a gold coin to hang on Grandpa's watch-chain, and a thin gold neck-chain for Grandma's locket.

And then it was time for Milly-Molly-Mandy and little-friend-Susan and Billy Blunt to give their presents.

They stood in a row, and Billy Blunt lifted his shovel-and-poker violin, and Milly-Molly-Mandy her comb-and-tissue-paper mouth-organ, and little-friend-Susan her saucepan-lid clappers; and they played and sang, hummed and clashed, *Happy Birthday to you!* only instead of "birthday" they sang, "Happy Golden Wedding to you!"

And then they shouted their own poem all together:

"Dear Grandpa and Grandma, we want to say
  We wish you a happy Golden Wedding Day.
  We want you to know our heart all burns
  To wish you Many Happy Returns.
  We hope you like our little stunt,
  From Milly-Molly-Mandy, Susan,
        and Billy Blunt!"

Grandpa and Grandma were nearly over-come, and everybody clapped as the three gave their presents then: two long yellow pen-cils with brass ends (which looked like gold) from little-friend-Susan; two "Golden-Glam-our Sachets" from Billy Blunt; and a little gold bell to ring whenever they wanted her from Milly-Molly-Mandy.

Grandpa and Grandma WERE pleased!

There was quite a bit of talk over Billy Blunt's sachets, though, as he had thought they were scent sachets, but the others said they were shampoos for golden hair, and, of course Grandpa's and Grandma's hair was white!

However, Grandma said her sachet smelled so delicious she would keep it among her handkerchiefs, and Grandpa could do the same with his. So that was all right.

Then they had tea, and Grandpa and Grandma cut big slices of their Golden Wedding cake, with a shiny gilt heart for everybody.

Afterwards Grandpa made quite a long speech. But all Grandma could say was that she thought such a lovely Golden Wedding was well worth waiting fifty years for!

So then Milly-Molly-Mandy and little-friend-Susan and Billy Blunt knew they had really and truly helped in making it such a splendid occasion!

MILLY-MOLLY-MANDY
HAS A SURPRISE

ONCE UPON A TIME Milly-Molly-Mandy was helping Mother to fetch some pots of jam down from the little storeroom.

Father and Mother and Grandpa and Grandma and Uncle and Aunty and Milly-Molly-Mandy between them ate quite a lot of jam, so Mother (who made all the jam) had to keep the pots upstairs because the kitchen cupboard wouldn't hold them all.

The little storeroom was up under the thatched roof, and it had a little square window very near to the floor, and the ceiling sloped away on each side so that Father or Mother or Grandpa or Grandma or Uncle or Aunty could stand upright only in the very middle of the room. (But Milly-Molly-Mandy could stand upright anywhere in it.)

When Mother and Milly-Molly-Mandy had found the jams they wanted (strawberry jam and blackberry jam and ginger jam), Mother looked round the little storeroom and said, "It's a pity I haven't got somewhere else to keep my jam-pots!"

And Milly-Molly-Mandy said, "Why, Mother, I think this is a very nice place for jam-pots to live in!"

And Mother said, "Do you?"

But a few days later Father and Mother went up to the little storeroom together and took out all the jam-pots and all the shelves that held the jam-pots and Father stood them down in the new shed he was making outside the back door, while Mother started cleaning out the little storeroom.

Milly-Molly-Mandy helped by washing the little square window – "So that my jam-pots can see out!" Mother said.

The next day Milly-Molly-Mandy came upon Father in the barn, mixing colour-wash in a bucket. It was a pretty colour, just like a pale new primrose, and Milly-Molly-Mandy dabbled in it with a bit of stick for a while, and then she asked what it was for.

And Father said, "I'm going to do over the walls and ceiling of the little storeroom with it." And then he added, "Don't you think it will make the jam-pots feel nice and cheerful?"

And Milly-Molly-Mandy said she was sure the jam-pots would just love it! (It was such fun!)

A little while afterwards Mother sent Milly-Molly-Mandy to the village to buy a packet of green dye at Mr Smale the Grocer's shop. And then Mother dyed some old casement curtains a bright green for the little storeroom window. "Because," said Mother, "the window looks so bare from outside."

And while she was about it she said she might as well dye the coverlet on Milly-Molly-Mandy's little cot-bed (which stood in one corner of Father's and Mother's room), as the pattern had washed nearly white. So Milly-Molly-Mandy had a nice new bedspread, instead of a faded old one.

The next Saturday, when Grandpa came home from market, he brought with him in the back of the pony-trap a little chest of drawers, which he said he had "picked up cheap." He thought it might come in useful for keeping things in, in the little storeroom.

And Mother said, yes, it would come in very useful indeed. So (as it was rather shabby) Uncle, who had been painting the door of the new shed with apple-green paint, painted the little chest of drawers green too, so that it was a very pretty little chest of drawers indeed.

"Well," said Uncle, "that ought to make any jam-pot taste sweet!"

Milly-Molly-Mandy began to think the little storeroom would be almost too good just for jam-pots.

Then Aunty decided she and Uncle wanted a new mirror in their room, and she asked Mother if their little old one couldn't be stored up in the little storeroom. And when Mother said it could, Uncle said he might as well use up the last of the green paint, so that he could throw away the tin. So he painted the frame of the mirror green, and it looked a very pretty little mirror indeed.

"Jam-pots don't want to look at themselves," said Milly-Molly-Mandy. She thought the mirror looked much too pretty for the little storeroom.

"Oh well – a mirror helps to make the room lighter," said Mother.

Then Milly-Molly-Mandy came upon Grandma embroidering a pretty little wool bird on either end of a strip of coarse linen. It was a robin, with a brown back and a scarlet front. Milly-Molly-Mandy thought it *was* a pretty cloth: and she wanted to know what it was for.

And Grandma said, "I just thought it would look nice on the little chest of drawers in the little storeroom." And then she added, "It might amuse the jam-pots!"

And Milly-Molly-Mandy laughed, and begged Grandma to tell her what the pretty cloth really was for. But Grandma would only chuckle and say it was to amuse the jam-pots.

The next day, when Milly-Molly-Mandy came home from school, Mother said, "Milly-Molly-Mandy, we've got the little storeroom in order again. Now, would you please run up and fetch me a pot of jam?"

Milly-Molly-Mandy said, "Yes, Mother. What sort?"

And Father said, "Blackberry."

And Grandpa said, "Marrow-ginger."

And Grandma said, "Red-currant."

And Uncle said, "Strawberry."

And Aunty said, "Raspberry."

But Mother said, "Any sort you like, Milly-Molly-Mandy!"

Milly-Molly-Mandy thought something funny must be going to happen, for Father and Mother and Grandpa and Grandma and Uncle and Aunty all looked as if they had got a laugh down inside them. But she ran upstairs to the little storeroom.

And when she opened the door, ...she saw...

Her own little cot-bed with the green coverlet on, just inside. And the little square window with the green curtains blowing in the wind. And a yellow pot of nasturtiums on the sill. And the little green chest of drawers with the robin cloth on it. And the little green mirror hanging on the primrose wall, with Milly-Molly-Mandy's own face reflected in it.

And then Milly-Molly-Mandy knew that the little storeroom was to be her very own little bedroom, and she said, "Oh-h-h-h!" in a very

She said, "Oh-h-h-h!" in a very hushed voice

hushed voice, as she looked all round her room.

Then suddenly she tore downstairs back into the kitchen, and just hugged Father and Mother and Grandpa and Grandma and Uncle and Aunty; and they all said she was their favourite jam-pot and pretended to eat her up!

And Milly-Molly-Mandy didn't know how to wait till bedtime, because she was so eager to go to sleep in the little room that was her Very Own!

MILLY-MOLLY-MANDY
GOES TO A PARTY

ONCE UPON A TIME something very nice
happened in the village where Milly-Molly-
Mandy and her Father and Mother and
Grandpa and Grandma and Uncle and Aunty
lived. Some ladies clubbed together to give a
party to all the children in the village, and of
course Milly-Molly-Mandy was invited.

Little-friend-Susan had an invitation too,
and Billy Blunt (whose father kept the corn-
shop where Milly-Molly-Mandy's Uncle got
his chicken feed), and Jilly, the little niece of
Miss Muggins (who kept the shop where
Milly-Molly-Mandy's Grandma bought her
knitting-wool), and lots of others whom Milly-
Molly-Mandy knew.

It was exciting.

Milly-Molly-Mandy had not been to a real party for a long time, so she was very pleased and interested when Mother said, "Well, Milly-Molly-Mandy, you must have a proper new dress for a party like this. We must think what we can do."

So Mother and Grandma and Aunty thought together for a bit, and then Mother went to the big wardrobe and rummaged in her bottom drawer until she found a most beautiful white silk scarf, which she had worn when she was married to Father, and it was just wide enough to be made into a party frock for Milly-Molly-Mandy.

Then Grandma brought out of her best handkerchief box a most beautiful lace handkerchief, which would just cut into a little collar for the neck of the party frock.

And Aunty brought out of her small top drawer some most beautiful pink ribbon, all smelling of lavender – just enough to make into a sash for the party frock.

And then Mother and Aunty set to work to cut and stitch at the party frock, while Milly-Molly-Mandy jumped up and down and handed pins when they were wanted.

The next day Father came in with a paper parcel for Milly-Molly-Mandy bulging in his coat pocket, and when Milly-Molly-Mandy unwrapped it she found the most beautiful little pair of red shoes inside!

And then Grandpa came in and held out his closed hand to Milly-Molly-Mandy, and when Milly-Molly-Mandy got his fingers open she found the most beautiful little coral necklace inside!

And then Uncle came in, and he said to Milly-Molly-Mandy, "What have I done with my handkerchief?" And he felt in all his pockets. "Oh, here it is!" And he pulled out the most beautiful little handkerchief with a pink border, which of course Milly-Molly-Mandy just knew was meant for her, and she wouldn't let Uncle wipe his nose on it, which he pretended he was going to do!

Milly-Molly-Mandy was so pleased she hugged everybody in turn – Father, Mother, Grandpa, Grandma, Uncle and Aunty.

At last the great day arrived, and little-friend-Susan, in her best spotted dress and silver bangle, called for Milly-Molly-Mandy, and they went together to the village institute, where the party was to be.

There was a lady outside who welcomed them in, and there were more ladies inside who helped them to take their things off. And everywhere looked so pretty, with garlands of coloured paper looped from the ceiling, and everybody in their best clothes.

Most of the boys and girls were looking at a row of toys on the mantelpiece, and a lady explained that they were all prizes, to be won by the children who got the most marks in the games they were going to have. There was a lovely fairy doll and a big teddy bear and a picture-book and all sorts of things.

And at the end of the row was a funny little white cotton-wool rabbit with a pointed paper hat on his head. And directly Milly-Molly-Mandy saw him she wanted him dreadfully badly, more than any of the other things.

Little-friend-Susan wanted the picture-book, and Miss Muggins' niece, Jilly, wanted the fairy doll. But the black, beady eyes of the little cotton-wool rabbit gazed so wistfully at Milly-Molly-Mandy that she determined to try ever so hard in all the games and see if she could win him.

Then the games began, and they were fun! They had a spoon-and-potato race, and musical chairs, and putting the tail on the donkey blindfold, and all sorts of guessing games.

And then they had supper – bread-and-butter with coloured hundreds-and-thousands sprinkled on, and red jellies and yellow jellies, and cakes with icing and cakes with cherries, and lemonade in red glasses.

It was quite a proper party.

And at the end the names of prize-winners were called out, and the children had to go up and receive their prizes.

At last the great day arrived

And what do you think Milly-Molly-Mandy got?

Why, she had tried so hard to win the little cotton-wool rabbit that she won first prize instead, and got the lovely fairy doll! And Miss Muggins' niece Jilly, who hadn't won any of the games, got the little cotton-wool rabbit with the sad, beady eyes – for do you know, the cotton-wool rabbit was only the booby prize, after all!

It was a lovely fairy doll, but Milly-Molly-Mandy was sure Miss Muggins' Jilly wasn't loving the booby rabbit as it ought to be loved, for its beady eyes did look so sad, and when she got near Miss Muggins' Jilly she stroked the booby rabbit, and Miss Muggins' Jilly stroked the fairy doll's hair.

Then Milly-Molly-Mandy said, "Do you love the fairy doll more than the booby rabbit?"

And Miss Muggins' Jilly said, "I should think so!"

So Milly-Molly-Mandy ran up to the lady who had given the prizes, and asked if she and Miss Muggins' Jilly might exchange prizes, and the lady said, "Yes, of course."

So Milly-Molly-Mandy and the booby rabbit went home together to the nice white cottage with the thatched roof, and Father and Mother and Grandpa and Grandma and Uncle and Aunty all liked the booby rabbit very much indeed.

And do you know, one day one of his little bead eyes dropped off, and when Mother had stuck it on again with a dab of glue, his eyes didn't look a bit sad any more, but almost as happy as Milly-Molly-Mandy's own!

The Nice White Cottage with the Thatched Roof (where Milly-Molly-Mandy lives)

The Brook

The Barn

Short Cut to School (only used in dry weather)

The Moggs' Cottage (where little-friend-Susan and Baby Moggs live)

To the Next Village

MAP of th

Joyce L. Brisley